PERFECT

C000038367

The Watchm.

by

Adesola Olagundoye

Published by

Kratos publishers

PERFECT PERCEPTION

Copyright ©2019 by Adesola Olagundoye

ISBN: 9781093453102

**PUBLISHED BY
KRATOS PUBLISHERS**

CONTENT PAGE

LIGHT IN THE MIDST............................. 4

PEARL FAMILY...................................... 6

OBSERVATORY WONDER................................ 8

TRUTH AND KNOWLEDGE............................. 15

DREAM OF FOOLS................................... 17

INSUFFICIENT WORSHIP............................. 21

DEATH AND LEGACY................................ 23

BATTLE AGAINST FALSEHOOD........................ 25

FORGOTTEN REALITY............................... 29

LOVE UNCONTAINABLE.............................. 31

ANGEL OR DEVIL'S COUSIN......................... 35

CONFUSION....................................... 40

REPENTANCE...................................... 45

Light in the midst

The darkness gave way to the light of the sun and so the despair of confusion gave way to the hope of clarity.

As the answer to a question that has stood in the chamber of discovery in the heart and mind of one who continually is not satisfied with welcoming the strange visitor until they walk into the room of delight, a delight that can only come from understanding and wisdom. If I were to light a candle on the top of the Mountain that stands as a beautiful giant at a distance of approximately two hundred miles from the balcony of my grandfather's mansion, would the darkness of the mountain be less dark, because of the candle? Or would the light of the candle be irrelevant to the darkness of the beautiful sleeping giant? Does more light change how I see the mountain? Does a light that cannot enlighten any darkness be relevant to the sight of the one looking? Do I need other sets of eyes to see the little champion of a candle burn gloriously? Or does it take light like that of the sun to make the sleeping giant wake with a beauty that is not known with the moon light?

Visitor after visitor kept wondering into an open door of the chambers of discovery in the heart of one that was born in a time when the sun was not shining and the bloom of the sun flower was fading gloriously to give way into a season, when the streets are filled with love from the multitudes of friends that have learnt to give their life for the next generation of growth, a growth that can only take place when the season was over.

Pearl family

Michael was a man born into a family that considered themselves to be a pearl of the community, precious in the sight of all who saw them as they truly were but not in the sight of them that saw them as they thought they ought to be. Michael's reasoning was due to many factors but of all the reasons for his reasons, his grandfather the watch maker had a profound impact on his meaning centre in the depths of his heart.

Whiles Michael's father was always wanting to spend time with his own son, the business of money making found a way of stealing the time that rightfully belonged to his son.

The grandson of the watchmaker picked up some habits from seeing his grandfather making and fixing watches. In the mind of the 5-year-old, his grandfather was the author of time itself and so made devices that helps the very interesting variety of people that came into his grandfather's mystery time room, at least that is what he called it. In the mind of the young prodigy, the creation of time and the measurement of time must have the same author, for who but the creator of a thing can know its true measure? For Michael's seventh birthday his grandfather gave him a gift, he came to believe is as important as life itself.

His very own watch, now he thought he could measure his own time and record his achievements in the time measured by his grandfather's gift of life. Every time he saw his grandfather, he saw the one who made time and measures it and makes for the very interesting people who came into his grandfather's mystery room.

Observatory wonder

One day when he came back from observing the time it took for his mother, a woman whom he saw as the kindest and most gracious person alive. To cook the wonderful breakfast; of toast, bacon, eggs, beans, butter, milk, some jam and some lovely hot chocolate. A thought began to rise inside his mind that the old lad, looked quite different yesterday than he did since his seventh birthday, does the passing of time change people? Or do people change in time, he thought? This led to a merry search for the understanding of human life and at the young age of 8 years; he spent 3 hours everyday understanding human growth, he did so for 30 days. After 90 hours of study which seemed to him like a lifetime of reading. He concluded that what he had imagined about the creator of time, no longer existed.

The next time he saw his grandfather, he thought to himself, 'grandad doesn't look as mysterious as I saw him 300 hours ago', in his obsession with time, he had kept track of every hour passing since he last saw his grandfather.

On the sight of his grandfather he realised the change that took place inside of him, was that he no longer believed his grandfather was the creator of time nor the author of his measurement, and more disappointing, that he had learnt the skill of making watches from a man who he thought, was grossly looking.

His grandfather deals with people every day and quickly noticed the change in the eyes of his lovely grandson and asked him what was wrong?

With tears the grandson said; you are not the author of time or its measurements, expecting the old man to convince him that he was and restore the mystery around his face but instead, a new mystery rose from the grandfather's face, one the boy has never really noticed before. The watchmaker's expression with raised eyebrow and a smile that seemed to make the stars look dull. Reflected the light of humility on the heart of a boy that seem to wonder about the identity of his being.

"No, I am not."

Responded the grandfather.

"But why have you never denied that you were not the creator of time or its measurements?"

"Because I am one of the creators of time and its measurements,"

Said the grandfather.

Now the mystery definitely returned on his grandfather's face, thought the young time inquisitor.

What do you mean grand-dad?

"See son, I believe we create our time within the time capsule and benefit a great deal from its measurements?"

"I don't follow," responded Michael.

See, there is a time for everything and right now we are having a time of knowledge, which we chose to create the very moment you began to seek for understanding my identity and I in turn, am trying to reveal my identity to you.

"Who are you grandad?"

"Hahahaha"

Now the old man was filled with a joy that seemed to have come from the depth of an ocean, with a remark that said, "that's my boy!"

See boy, my identity is complex and yet so simple, complex to those who have learnt to close their heart and simple to those that have their heart open.

Now, today's conversation will contribute to whether you will choose to be the one with a closed heart or the one with an open heart.

But ultimately you will make your choice and choose which sort you are in life.

As to my identity, I will reveal the aspect of me that has brought you to question who I am in a letter, that will be given to you on the day that I die.

Michael said to him, I now think of you as the mystery granddad.

This time the grand father's eyes seem to say one word: compassion.

The grandfather with what seems like honey in his mouth, said to him, by the time you read the letter you will realise you had known me all along and that the question that brought you to question who I am, could lead you to a greater truth of who I am, if you would let the question lead you towards, what is true in you and in me.

"What is true in you and in me" asked the boy to his grandfather?

Now the look on his grandfather's face seemed to be like a river that gushes out in light brighter than the sun.

Grandfather responded;

"Many things are true in you and in me,"

"But the deepest things that are true in you and in me is that I will always be your grandfather and I will always love you, and I know you too will always love me."

The words seemed to bring life into the heart of the young man, he looked down thinking there was a drizzle of rain coming, but realised the water was from his face, then saw that he was engulfed in what he was sure was a type of love that he knew was pure love, if ever he felt purity, he felt known by his grandfather.

Again, his grandfather looked so different every time he sees him, he saw him in a more beautiful way than the creator of time and its measurements but saw him as his grandfather that loved him.

The watch maker had changed the world of a boy from that of scientific uncertainty into that of invisible delight, from that of darkness where there was doubt and what seemed like betrayal, to that of light where there is knowledge, trust and truth.

Truth and knowledge

It was this truth and knowledge of love that Michael used as the tape measure and scale for denoting that his father's love for money was greater than his father's love for him. Which at first led to a lack in self confidence in the heart of the young boy and then turned to anger, especially seeing that His father looked more fulfilled whiles talking about his accomplishments and riches than he did, his wife and child.

He wasn't the only child of his parents, but his little sister died of a sickness that wasn't fully discoverable in the time she was born. It was from this time specifically that Michael, when he saw his father realised that something different was at play in the engine that kept his father's heart running.

Michael's father Stephen was a man that was very in love with his father, and mother, to him they seemed like one soul living in two bodies. He was constantly nurtured by the way his mother spoke about his father with constant reverence and awe. To him, his father was a hero, a man to look up to..., to become an ideal for the world. The words of his father were to him like the very words of God himself.

Dream of fools

Until he noticed one day his father's delight in the watches, and how the people admired him for the work that he offered them.

The question came, do people love my father simply because he is a watch maker? Or do they love my father because he loves to make watches?

This question consumed him to such a point that he began to dream of it, and he dreamt, that he was an Aerospace engineer and was just as skilled has his father was in making watches, in making space crafts and understanding the mystery of flight.

The people came and spoke about him with awe and reverence, the same awe and reference he thought he saw in his mother's eye when she saw his father.

Awaking from the dream, he was drunk with a wine of false worship, that had come from the men and women in his dream, and from that day forward he sought to become the idol of the men and women he saw in his dreams, and moved further away from the hero he once had.

Had he known the men and women in his dream would have called his beloved father a loser and found him abominable to be celebrated by the world. A man not to become, a scum of society.

The change in Stephen's attitude, was quickly noticed by his mother and was later on confirmed by his father, that the confidence that was once pure was now soiled with arrogance and pride.

And when asked who his hero is? Stephen's response was, "a man greater than his father!"

After all, father's want their children to be greater.

It was obvious that when that sentence came from the mouth of his father, it was hope and faith, but when it came from the mouth of the son, it was arrogance and pride.

This might have been the only one mistake the watchmaker made but it was very costly, he did not discipline Stephen with the right measure, to get to the root of his pride and arrogance but tried to cut the fruit from the tree of a dream of fools. His aim should have been for the dream itself.

Like all false idols, this dream was now buried in the deepest corner of Stephen's heart and became the engine that made his heart work.

No matter how many times the watchmaker told his son of the deep love he had for him, the son was more in love with the idea of becoming greater than his father. Somehow when his father told him "I love you", In his heart he loved the idol that the men and women from his dream had worshipped.

His response to his dad was.

"I know father, and I won't let you down".

The look on his father's face was that of concern.

The type of concern that only true love can understand but in more clear terms, he was concerned that his son could take a simple truth of 'I love you' and turn it into a requirement of performance for life.

He tried many a time to explain to his son what he meant by his love, but his words where like pouring water to the back of a cup. For his son was consumed with the idol of himself that was revealed to him from a dream of fools.

Stephen is Michael's father, in his heart he has embraced as light what truly is darkness and embraced as truth what truly is a lie. The lie was that 'his father loved watches more than him and that is what made his father great'. So, he pursued to become the father he thought his dad was. Unfortunately, he became the lie that he pursued passionately.

Insufficient worship

When his daughter died, his passion for aerospace no longer was enough to fill the void inside the heart. The idol that he had set up was no longer sufficient to comfort or bring any meaning or purpose to his existence, he even considered suicide.

For in his heart he was a failure and had never been able to attain to the glory of his watchmaker father. Even though he had the praise of man, it wasn't quite like the dream had shown him.

It wasn't quite the type of awe and reverence he saw in the eyes of his mother when she looked at his father. So, he saw that people loved money a great deal and that if he became the richest, then he would have the look of adoration. Thankfully, he is an aerospace engineer.

He sold some patents and designs, and made millions, no matter the extent of the praise and exaltation of man, he realised the type of glory his father had was of the greater kind. Though he became richer and greater in the eyes of man, he knew in his heart that he was lesser and much further away from the type of man his father was. Never saw the same look in the eyes of his wife or children.

When his daughter Evelyn died, the world stopped and he realised he had wasted his time in pursuit of things that was not profitable. So, he hated himself and was incapable of showing love, which was what Michael perceived in his father.

The pain of knowing that he wasn't loved as much from his father, left a void in Michael's heart, if not for the words and love of his grandfather, Michael too would have gone on a journey not profitable for himself.

Death and Legacy

After a few years the watchmaker died and left letters to both his son and grandson and all the members of his family. He died at the age of 100 years old and left such a legacy that can only be appropriately described as glorious. And it's a type of glory that doesn't fade. The eulogy of the mum was like the oracles of God. Describing the selfless warrior, the undying love, and the man she said she was more than honoured to call her husband.

Stephen thought,

'if he were to die, would his wife speak in the same way?'

Michael thought, 'if the selfless warrior was so great, how comes his son turned out incapable of loving selflessly?'

Therefore, as life would have it, he too began to turn away from the path that the grandfather had walked, as the pain of a father incapable of loving like his father, was too great.

Not knowing it is when we have judged others wrongly that we have opened the door to falsehood in our own lives.

Battle against falsehood

It was after the grandfather's death that Michael's thought patterns began to divulge from the place of the truth he knew about his grandfather, to the place where he considered nothing to be true anymore.

Due to his very mysterious upbringing at the watchmaker's mystery room, he found solace in nature and usually loves staying in gardens or parks.

In the middle of summer in a lovely sunny day, a day that decides to change the story of the young time inquisitor forever.

Due to his background in time observation, one thing Michael had learnt is that each day brings its own mystery but since the death of his grandfather, it seemed to him it brought more sorrow and a longing for something that was more real, something like his grandfather had.

In the midst of his thoughts, there seemed to be an interruption with the most lovely voice, he thought, that seemed like that of angels, for a second he thought he had died and gone to heaven, to see his grandfather or so, but far from it, in the midst of the velvet roses, and yellow daffodils, and a gentle summer breeze, a song with words as such:

'If love was just a song, no words to tell you how I feel,

If love was just a song, no melodies to tell you that I love you.

If love was just a song, then I will never stop singing forever'.

His heart seemed to shed tears at the sound and genuity of the voice of an angel, he thought to himself, but out from the most lovely scenery springs a woman so beautiful to behold, the kind that you paint and put in a gallery, he thought to himself. It was from this time forward where mystery became misery. When he thought about love, he couldn't help but think of the beautiful woman singing amidst the flowers and many times would answer to the woman's song in his heart.

'If there are no words to tell me how you feel, if love was my song, no words would hide themselves to show you how I feel.

No melodies to tell you that I love you. If love was my song, I will search heaven and hell to find the suitable melodies to tell you my love for you.

 If love was my song, then I will bring forever into this very moment to sing the song to you.

In his head they were a match made in heaven, she was wearing a beautiful red dress and had a face that he thought was veiled by the sound of her voice and beauty that simply made the thoughts in his head stop.

The thought of speaking to her terrified him, but it wasn't a fear that shut him down, it was a kind of fear that wakes one up to the possibilities of an eternity with such endless wonder.

This imagination soon became an ongoing longing for something that seemed so far out of reach, which began to make him wear away physically.

He sometimes forgot to eat, he had created this perfect world for himself and this lovely nameless angel. Just like his father, he fell in love with the man who was in love with the nameless angel and he had imagined how this woman would also look to him and craved to become the man the nameless beauty loved.

Forgotten reality

Only in his case there was something quite odd about himself in his imagination, and in his heart, whenever he thought of his grandfather, the beauty of the nameless angel seemed to fade.

But like his father he too chose to forget the beauty that doesn't fade and swapped it with a beauty that fades, and after the nameless wonder he followed.

He found out her name was Irene, which means peace but like many woman who are very beautiful outwardly, she too had fought a fight to attain to inner beauty, she was most days on the winning side of an inner beauty but when she ever was on the losing side, it seemed all the beauty tend to dissipate into an abyss of nothingness and all that is left is physical beauty.

From the rising of the sun, Michael began to invent a way of acquiring Irene, so she could belong to him. Every time that thought came to his mind his grandfather would flash in his mind with the look, he once remembered but had now become a bit dim, as the glory of Irene had become brighter than that of the grandfather.

Just like all idolatry, taking the glory that only belongs to God and giving it to a man or animal or things.

However, he had an experience with his grandfather that always made him question his unreserved passion for Irene without knowing her.

So, he decided to know her and pursue her and surely, Irene was a woman that knew men that wanted her for her beauty or for herself. But she had given herself to so many men, she could hardly tell the difference between who is who and what is what.

Love uncontainable

Michael approached Irene and said "here, I wrote words to how I felt for you".

"Excuse me Mr, do I know you?"

"Yes, I am the man you couldn't tell how you felt in the garden?"

"Hmmmm."

"Am not sure I understand what you mean?"

Irene at this point was going to just ignore him and be rude to him, but for some reason the countenance of the odd creature seems to have a pleasantness that comes from a world she is not accustomed to.

"Read the words and you will understand", said the young romantic soldier.

She laughed him off and walked away with the note in her hands.

Into the corner of her room, as her house was not too far away from where Michael had met her.

So, she began reading;

Irene we may not know each other, but the possibility of knowing you, is worth risking my life for.

We may never have met, but just the thought of meeting you, is worth laying down my life for.

What I felt when I heard you sing in the garden, was what I had been searching for in my life.

You Irene, have become to me a treasure, that I would always cherish.

Should you read this letter and show no interest in me, I will be content with just the opportunity to hear you sing and to see you.

If after you read this nothing in your heart is awakened, then know that I have been waking up to you every morning for six months with your voice in my head.

I would be so honoured with just one hour of your time.

Yours truly Michael.

Irene being the hopeless romantic she was cried at the letter, first it was romance, then it was anger, then it was fear. Has he been following me she thought to herself?

She was going to meet him across the street and threating to call the police.

But as she came out of her house, there he was across the street.

An odd looking fellow with beautiful eyes and a countenance that says, "I will never leave you", she felt safe just looking at him.

Whiles she approached him to scorn him, she found herself accepting the invitation to the one hour with the most romantic man she thought she had met.

In her mind she began to wonder how she could fix up his clothing, should he be one who is intelligible and a man that is worthy of her, she would train him to become her man.

After all every man needs a woman's touch.

Out of her mouth, it was pride and arrogance.

Out of his mouth, it was love and romance.

Angel or devil's cousin

Irene's inner battle was confusion, for one day, she is the loveliest and the next day, she is the devil's cousin.

Michael seem to have got her on a lovely day. But to his utter ignorance not aware that the cousin comes for regular visits.

They met the next day at a café not too far from Irene's.

Her first question was, "have you been following me then?"

"Yes" he said,

"I knew it, you are a stalker"

"No,

Not like that,

I have been following you in my head,

my dream, my imagination"

"Oh, I see, so you are a dreamer then?"

"So, what does this dreamer do?"

"Well" he said, "I fix watches just like my grandfather."

Michael responded.

"How do you pay the bills?"

"Well the Job pays well Irene."

She asked him,

"Which garden did you hear me sing?"

"The matrix garden"

Michael responded.

"And? "

"Oh, pardon me ma'am?"

"Wow, you are well cultured already. "

Now Michael's former nameless angel, at this point already began to dissipate and grew two devilish horns in her head.

"Do you drink?"

"No Ma'am"

"Call me Irene" she said.

"Alright, No Irene."

"So, what do you want to know about me?"

"I want to know what makes you feel there can be no words to a love that you feel?"

She said, "I don't recall singing that song, but I sometimes sing spontaneous songs, that might have been one of them,"

The angel began to reappear in his mind.

It seemed like you were singing with no one looking. So, I got to see you like you truly are and it really, really really…….

Really what sir?

"Oh, my name is Michael"

"Oh yes, I saw from the letter. "

"I guess am trying to say that I was really undone. By such natural beauty, talking about the beauty of your heart."

"Sir, you do not know me!!"

"Why do you say such nice things about me?"

The question surprised Michael.

"Well, I was just trying to put words to how I felt," he responded.

And she began to cry.

"You can't just come here and tell me how you feel, when I have never met you in my life."

(The devil reappeared.)

But he said to her "I wasn't looking for such an impact or beauty, but it found me in the garden, and it happened to be you and if I didn't tell you how I felt, I thought I would die."

The more words that flowed from the mouth of the young warrior, the more the fences of self-protection in Irene began to crumble like the walls of Jericho.

Michael said, "I wasn't ready to see such honesty walking in the cool of the day. But it did and Irene if you would hear me, I want to tell you that I love you."

"How do you know that sir?"

She responded.

"Because I know it's true!"

But Irene walked out of the café, ecstatic, angry and not really knowing how to react to such pure and undiluted love, she thought it was all an act and that this type of man never existed. So, she walked out on him and never saw him again.

She went back to her old lovers and married a man, who she tolerated more than loved but felt this was a world she understood and could be herself.

Confusion

Michael was devastated, how could this happen? He loved her truly he said to himself.

He thought love was the basis for life. So, he turned his back on love, and when he did, again his grandfather flashed in his heart, but he kept his heart locked.

It was near winter, three months since Irene's wedding that Michael finally understood how bad his misery had gone. People didn't recognise him, he had fallen into self-pity and thought he was a victim of love, a victim of romance, a victim of preferring another.

He was about to move out of town when he saw his grandfather's letter, that was four years ago he said to himself.

"What possibly, can a dead man know about love."

And when he said that, he knew that what he had said was not true. And remembered the conversation he had with his grandfather. Like a piece of his mind finally returned to him after a vacation in hell.

When he now thought of Irene, he thought she was one of the falling angels sent to deceive him, he blamed his father, grand father and the whole world for allowing this kind of deception to happen to him. How could this be? How could evil be returned for good? How could hatred be returned for kindness? How could these things happen?

His returning thoughts made him curious to read his grandfather's letter, although he was in hopelessness and despair.

He tore open the letter and began reading:

Dear Michael,

'He cried'

As he felt his grandfather right there in the room with him.

Dear Michael,

I promised to reveal the truth about my identity when I die, and here is the truth about my identity. The truth about my identity is that you already know who I am, and know that I know who you are too, who I am will only be a mystery, if you close your heart to the belief that I love you, then I will only be to you the creator of time and measurements but If you open your heart to the belief that I love you, then you will see yourself in me. As you came from me as the child of my child you too are my child and therefore, I too am your father, you also bear the family name. If truly your heart is open when you are reading this, you should hear my voice speaking to you, deep in your heart. Even though, you do not see me, for not even time and measurements can stop love from touching the heart, pure selfless love like the day that I showed you what is true in you and what is true in me, is truly timeless as I am sure as you read this and remember that time, you can feel the very love flood your heart. You are in my image, I am sure you can see the resemblance, for true love will always expose falsehood, which if you ever find in yourself, know that it's a deviation from who you are.

And always try to return to the point of knowing that you are loved. This will always guide you to the ultimate truth about life. That life transcends the physical senses and is a great deal dependent on the state of your heart.

You will make mistakes, but this is the beauty of love, it doesn't just love when things are perfect but love, loves even when mistakes are made and when rejection and abandonment happen.

Love transcends all.

Love is the greatest, so always remember to love. When you don't find the strength to love, always remember that you are loved.

This will fill you with enough love to love even the very unlovable.

For in all my experience in making watches that measure time, love has been the most important thing to fill up time, which at least is what all my customers tell me.

I love you

Your Grandad

Watchmaker.

REPENTANCE

Michael's clothes at this point were soaked with tears, you would have thought he had just come from swimming in the nearby lake. He woke up every morning and cried for two weeks straight, it seems he never ran out of tears.

He lamented the fact that he walked off from a path that was so sure, and so firm to being deceived by what he now saw very clearly was selfishness.

For when he read the words of his grandfather about what was true in them both, he knew instantly that what was true about him and in Irene was selfishness. For love to be love two selfish people could not draw closer to each other.

He realised he was more concerned about the image he had made in his mind, than actually getting to know the true person Irene was and love her truly.

He realised that his closed heart had led him down a path that was not very profitable, but to the degree his heart was open was to the degree he was able to perceive true love.

And so, he wrote to Irene,

Dear Irene,

I must congratulate you on your wedding, I am glad you have found one that suits who you are, and I truly love you always. Sorry for any pain and misunderstanding I might have caused you and I was selfish in the way I approached you. I wish you all the best in everything that you do.

Your brother

Michael

He had realised what mistake he had made in allowing idolatry into his heart, how he had exchanged a glory that does not fade for one that does, once the glory is faded it becomes pretty useless.

His epiphany also helped his father come to some emotional healing, he spoke to his dad freely about how he had believed the lie from his own imagination and dream and had led to the greatest disappointment and how that is the destiny of all who live selfishly and think selfishly, it will always give a result that never satisfy and it pays a heavy toll.

His dad saw the truth about his son's experience and at this point had nothing to lose in asking for forgiveness, they became great friends.

It was at this point that Michael was considering about the perception of things.

How when he thought his grandfather had not been the creator of time it almost led to him thinking his grandfather was liar and betrayer.

But when love came into him, this made his grandfather look more glorious than the creator of time and measurements.

Also, how love had saved him from the depression of the deception he had fallen into, which made him realise that even the righteous fall, but love covers sin and restored the relationship with his father.

Overall, he realised for perception to be perfect, love needs to be present. Total selfless love and until we all attain to it like the watchmaker, our perception keeps growing.

But once we attain to pure selfless love, we attain a glory that never fades and are always alive in the hearts of the people who have received such love.

Michael found a woman in the most mysterious way, as time revealed itself, and her name was Unity, she gave Michael, two sons and a daughter.

With his wife asking him about Irene

He used the analogy of the candle in the mountain, it was light that had no relevance to the darkness of his life. Especially from His grandfather's mansion, meaning undying and unfading glory.

The Love he found with Unity was one that was like the sun and it brought out the hill in all its glory, especially from his grandfather's mansion. It had a type of glory that never faded.

Printed in Great Britain
by Amazon